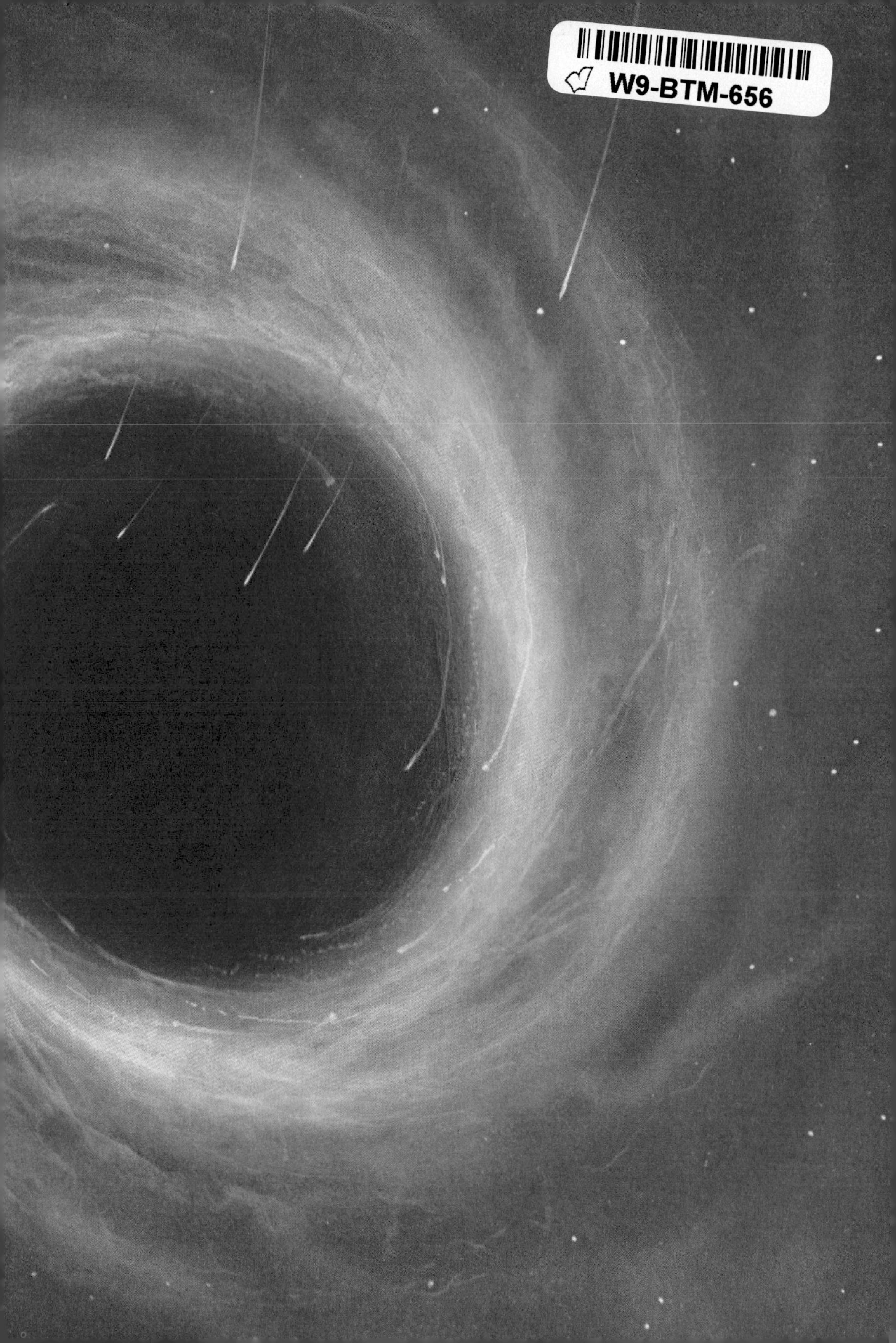
W9-BTM-656

WALT DISNEY PRODUCTIONS presents

Book Club Edition

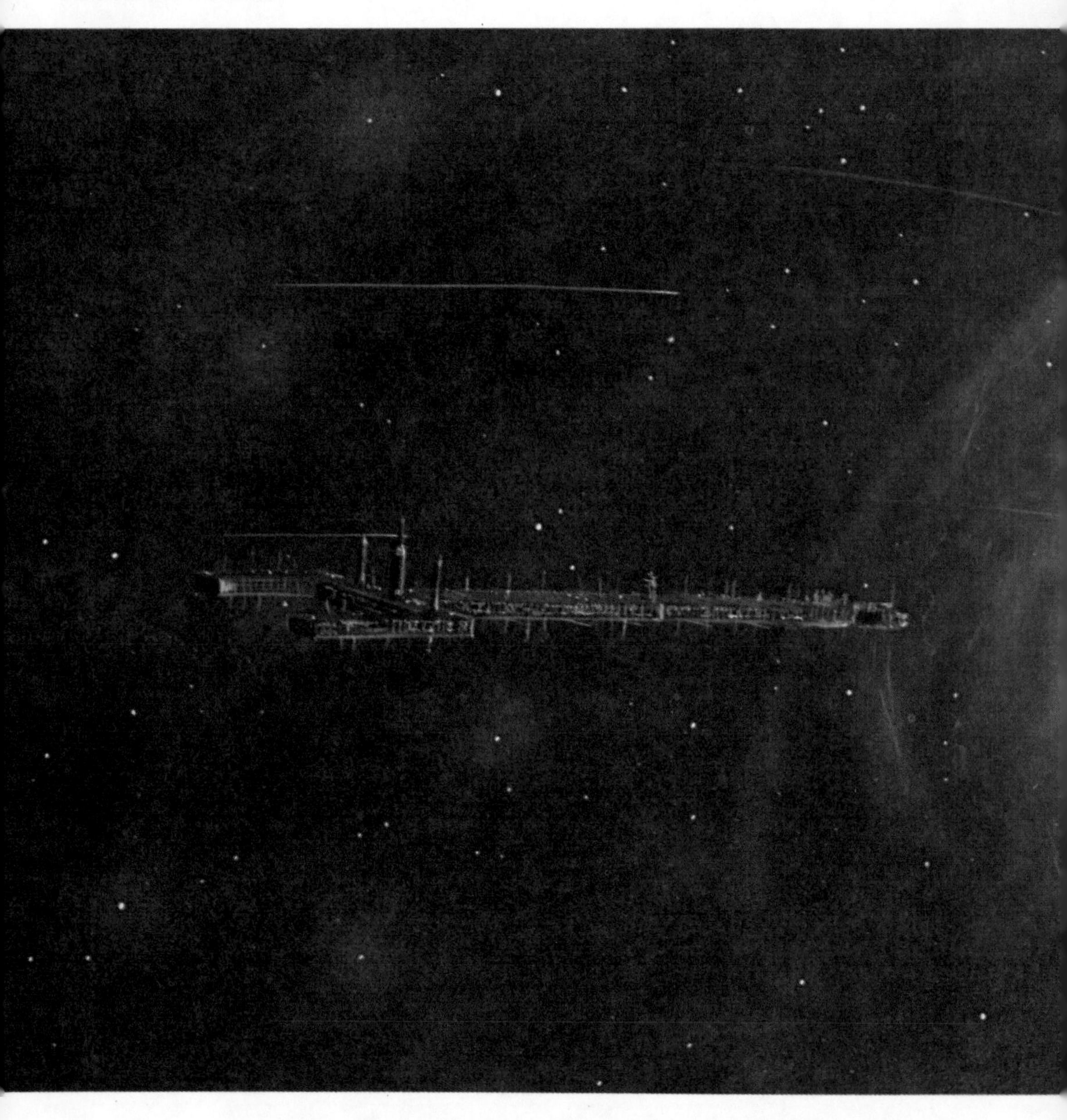

 Published in the United States by Random House, Inc., New York, and simultaneously in Canada by Random House of Canada Limited, Toronto. *Library of Congress Cataloging in Publication Data:* The black hole. (Walt Disney's wonderful world of reading) SUMMARY: While maintaining surveillance over a black hole, the crew of the spacecraft *Palomino* located a long-lost ship now manned by one human and an army of robots. [1. Black holes (Astronomy)–Fiction. 2. Robots–Fiction. 3. Science fiction] I. Disney (Walt) Productions. PZ7.B5315 [Fic] 79-10622 ISBN: 0-394-84279-0 (trade); 0-394-94279-5 (lib. bdg.). Manufactured in the United States of America. 1 2 3 4 5 6 7 8 9 0
A B C D E F G H I J K 9

Random House New York

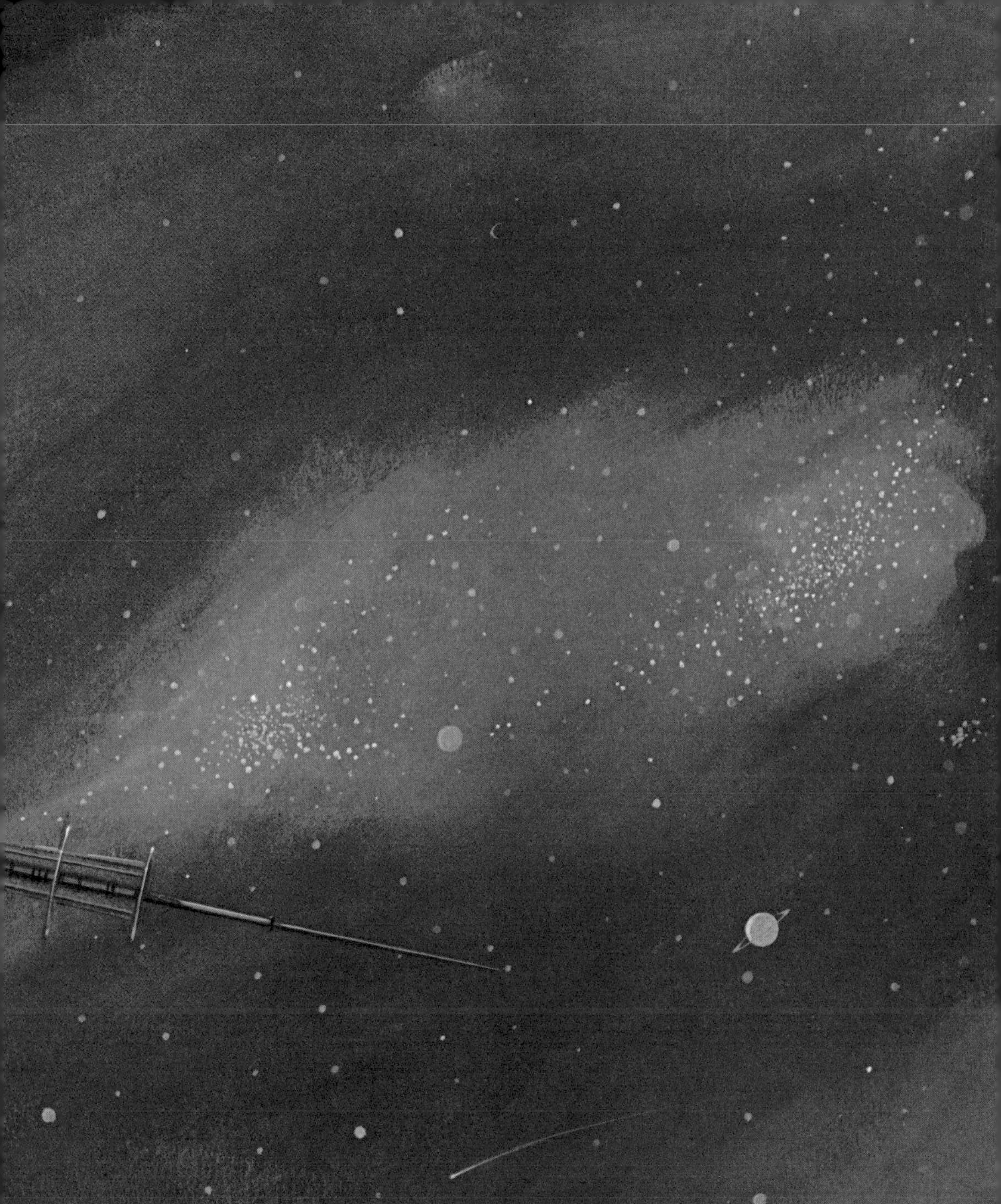

The spaceship *Palomino* was looking for life on other planets.

It had been in outer space for many months.

Now it was making the long trip home to earth.

Captain Holland and his mate, Mr. Pizer, were steering the ship.

V.I.N.CENT., a robot, and Dr. Kate were reading reports from the ship's computer.

DDA939
618406
123456789
2785335
F. LF. 396

Suddenly the computer reported a strange object in space.

V.I.N.CENT. pressed the viewer button.

A picture of the object appeared in the air.

V.I.N.CENT. and Dr. Kate called Captain Holland over to see it.

“It is a huge spaceship!” said Dr. Kate.

“But that is impossible,” said Captain Holland.

“No one builds ships that big anymore,” said V.I.N.CENT.

The old ship was called the *Cygnus*.

It had been lost in space many years before.

Now the ghost ship seemed to be floating close to a large black hole.

"How can it stay there?" V.I.N.CENT. asked. "A black hole sucks up everything that comes near it."

They brought their ship in for a closer look.

As the *Palomino* moved closer to the Black Hole, the ship began to shake all over.

It was the strong pull from the Black Hole.

Then a door in the ship blew open.

Emergency—the *Palomino* was losing air!

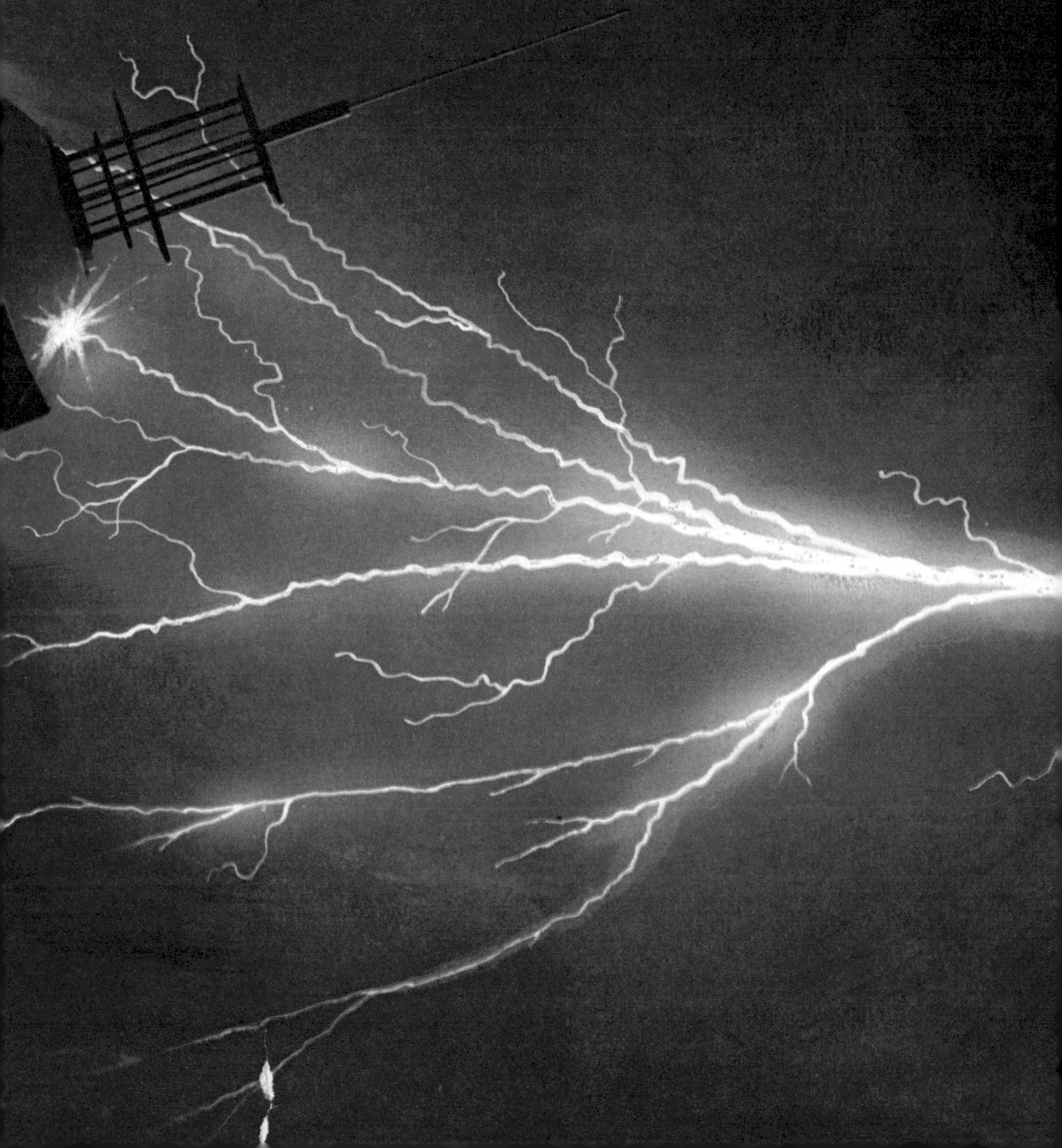

Mr. Pizer read a computer report and shook his head.

"That hatch has to be closed from the outside, and fast," he said. "Only V.I.N.CENT. can do it."

Dr. Kate helped V.I.N.CENT. get ready to go outside the ship.

"Be careful, old friend," she said.

"It is nice to have you worry about me," said V.I.N.CENT. "But I will be okay."

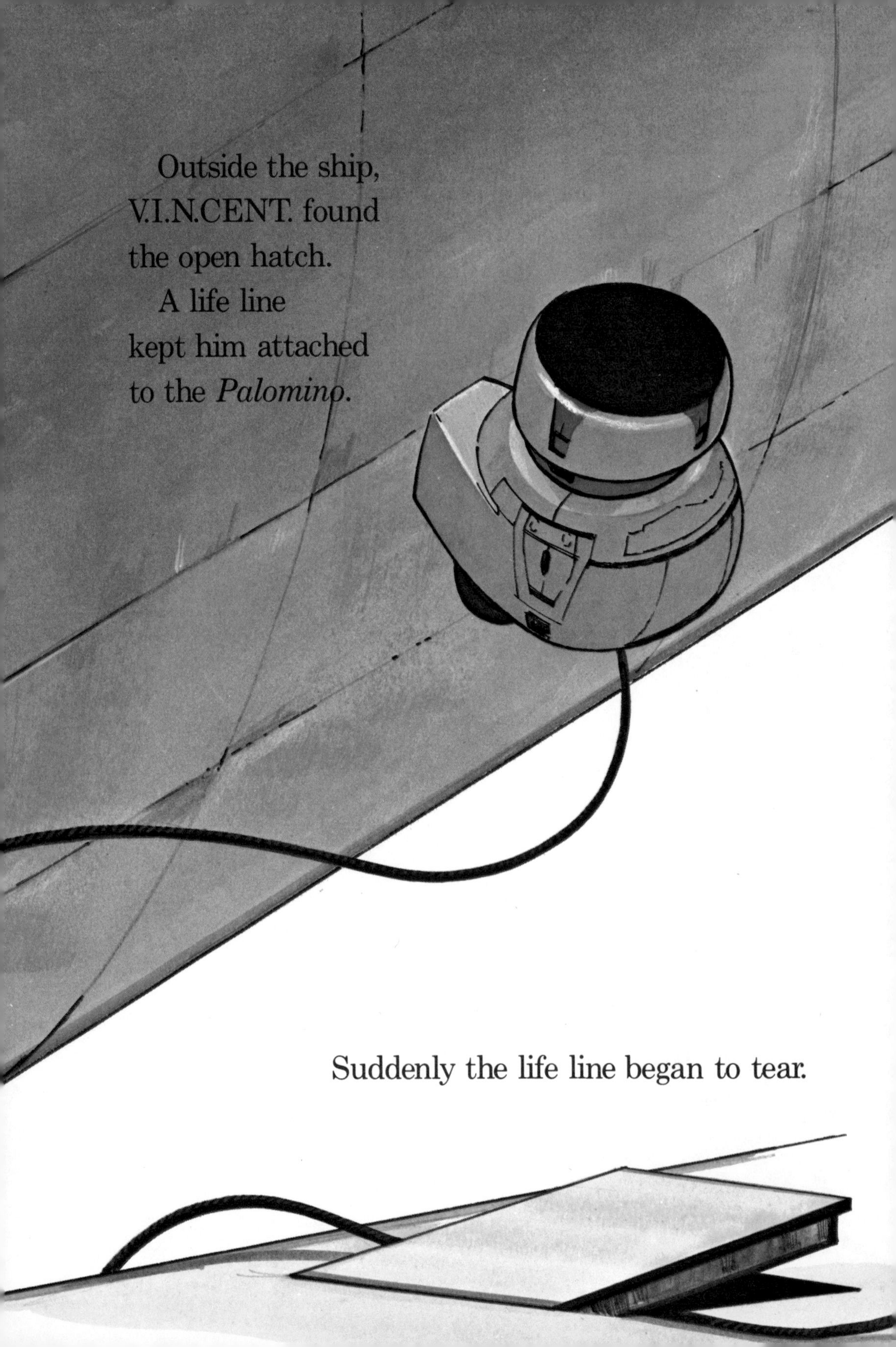

Outside the ship,
V.I.N.CENT. found
the open hatch.

A life line
kept him attached
to the *Palomino*.

Suddenly the life line began to tear.

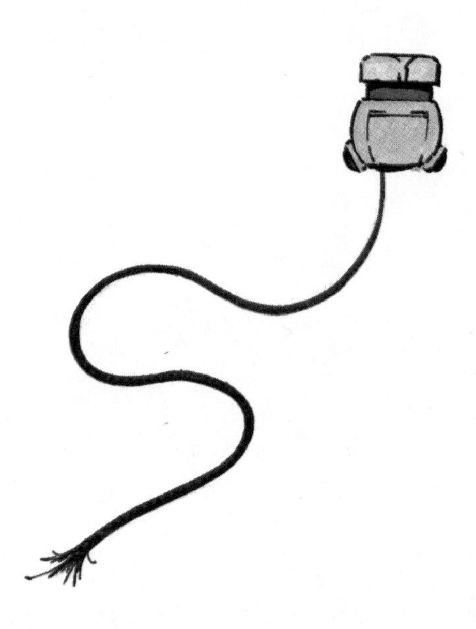

In seconds it snapped in two.

V.I.N.CENT. started to drift off into space.

VINCENT

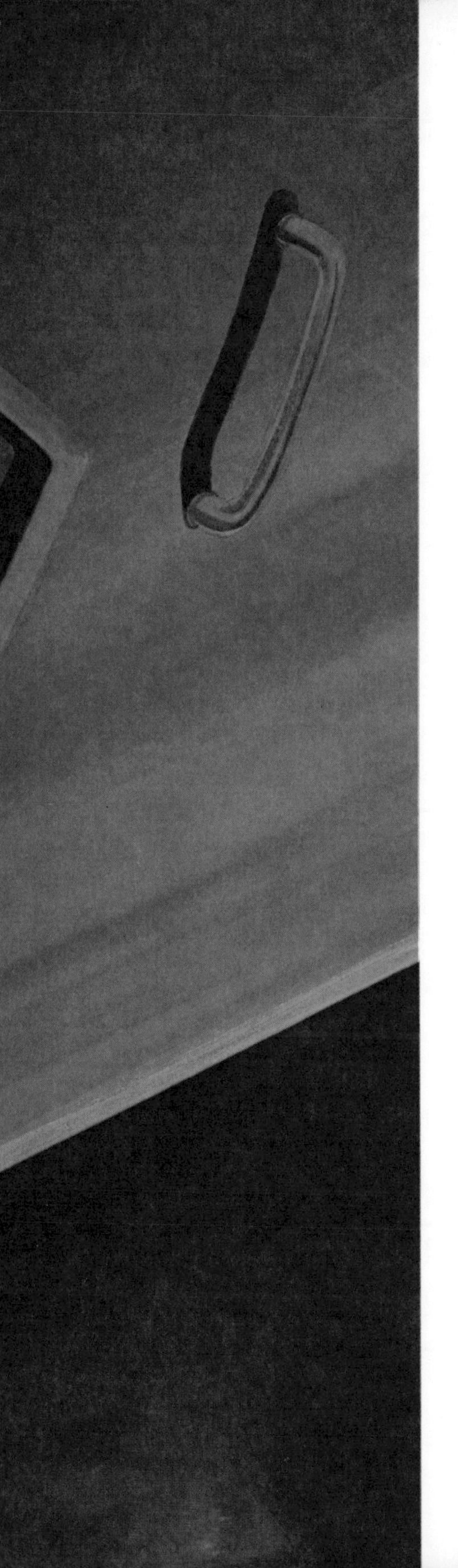

But V.I.N.CENT. had special tools in his robot body.

He quickly shot out a rescue line with a magnet on one end.

The magnet stuck to the metal ship.

V.I.N.CENT. pulled himself back to the *Palomino*.

Then he closed the open hatch.

There was damage inside the *Palomino,* too. The crew tried to make repairs, but it was too big a job.

Captain Holland looked at the *Cygnus* on his view screen.

"We have to try to land on that ship," he said. "Maybe we will find the parts there that we need. It is our only chance."

The little *Palomino* flew closer and closer to the giant *Cygnus*.

The old ship was more than a mile long.

The *Palomino* touched down.
The landing was perfect.

V.I.N.CENT. was there to meet them.

He had floated down from the *Palomino* and landed just ahead of them.

But they saw no one else when they went inside the huge, silent ship.

They had not gone far when they found an air car that still worked.

The four friends climbed in.

It carried them down a long hallway.

At last the air car stopped.

There stood the biggest robot the crew had ever seen!

His name was Maximillian.

The red robot led them to the ship's control center.

A man in a red suit stepped forward. He did not look friendly.

"I am Dr. Reinhardt," he said. "Why have you come aboard my ship?"

Captain Holland explained that they needed new parts to fix the *Palomino*.

"We can provide them," said Dr. Reinhardt. "Maximillian here will show you the way."

Dr. Kate stayed behind while Maximillian took Captain Holland, Mr. Pizer, and V.I.N.CENT. to the supply area.

It was a long way from the control center.

Dr. Reinhardt told Dr. Kate about his work.

"You have come at the perfect time," he said. "The small probe ship that I sent into the Black Hole is on its way back here now."

"That is crazy," said Dr. Kate. "Nothing comes back from a black hole."

On his view screen, Dr. Reinhardt showed Dr. Kate a picture of the probe ship.

"My next plan," he said, "is to take the *Cygnus* into the Black Hole. And you will come with me."

"You are a madman!" said Dr. Kate. "I won't go!"

Two robot soldiers came and grabbed her by the arms.

Dr. Reinhardt smiled.

Dr. Kate screamed.

"Keep her quiet," he said to the robots. "Do not let her leave the ship."

V.I.N.CENT. heard
Dr. Kate's screams.
He had to find her!

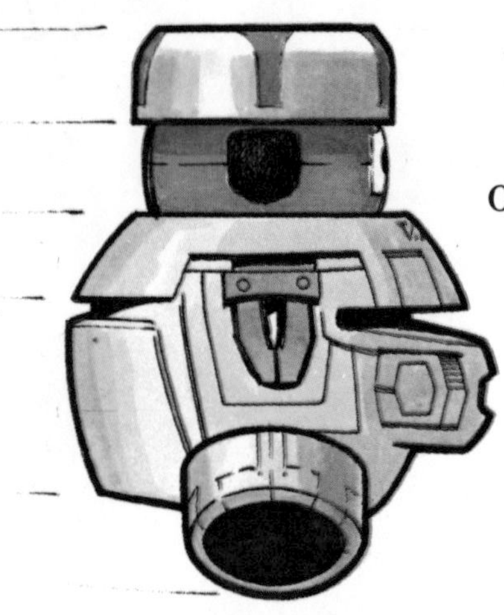

He zoomed down
one hallway . . .

. . . and up
another . . .

. . . but he could not
find her anywhere.

Then a friendly robot named Old B.O.B. stopped V.I.N.CENT.

"You must get Dr. Kate off this ship," Old B.O.B. said. "Dr. Reinhardt wants to take her with him on a trip into the Black Hole!"

"Come on," said V.I.N.CENT. "We have to tell Captain Holland."

V.I.N.CENT. and Old B.O.B. found Captain Holland. They told him about Dr. Reinhardt's plans.

The three hurried into a room where Dr. Kate was being held prisoner.

Captain Holland quickly helped her escape through the exit door.

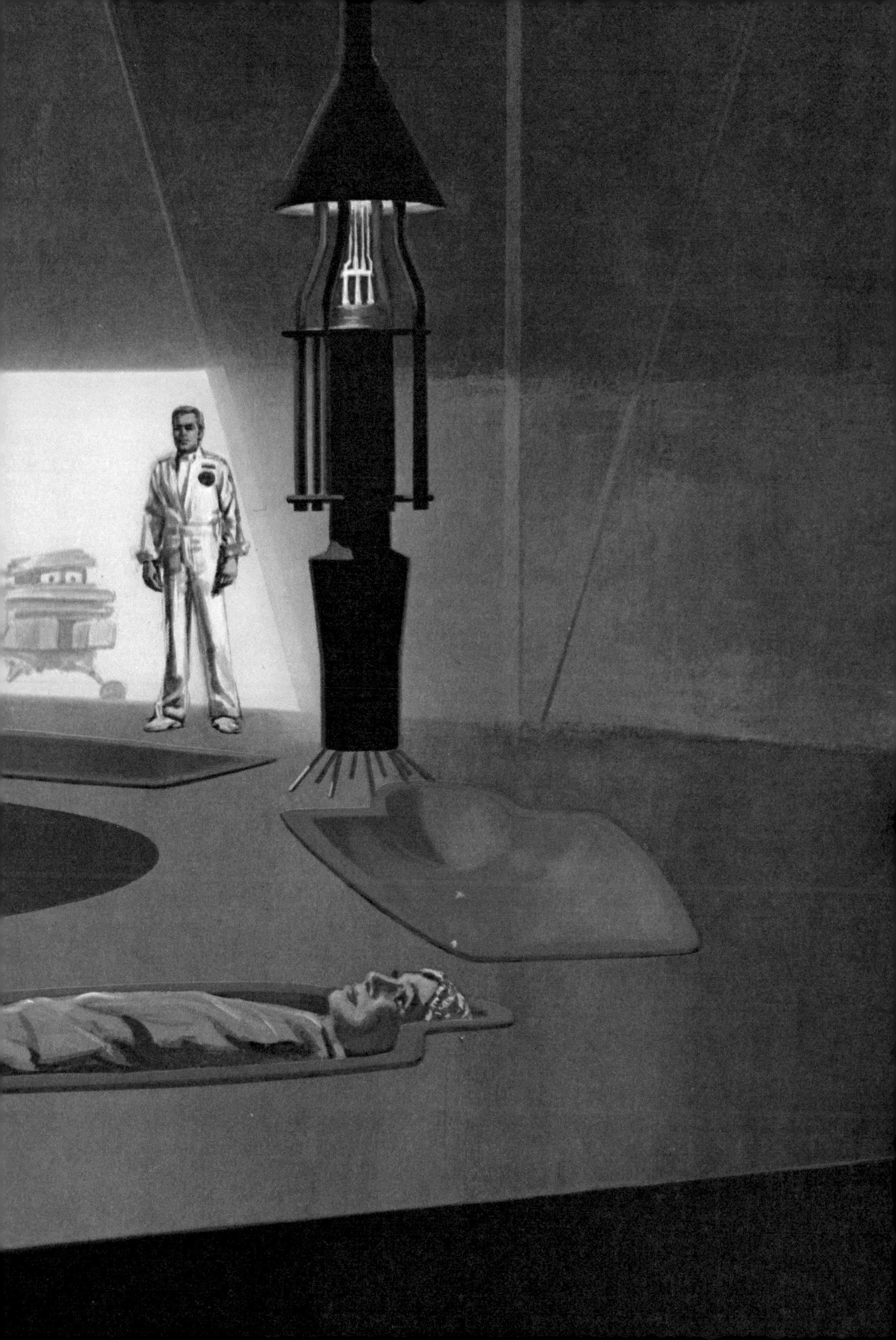

Just then Maximillian appeared and fired his laser gun at V.I.N.CENT.

V.I.N.CENT. dodged and fired back.

But the giant red robot kept coming.

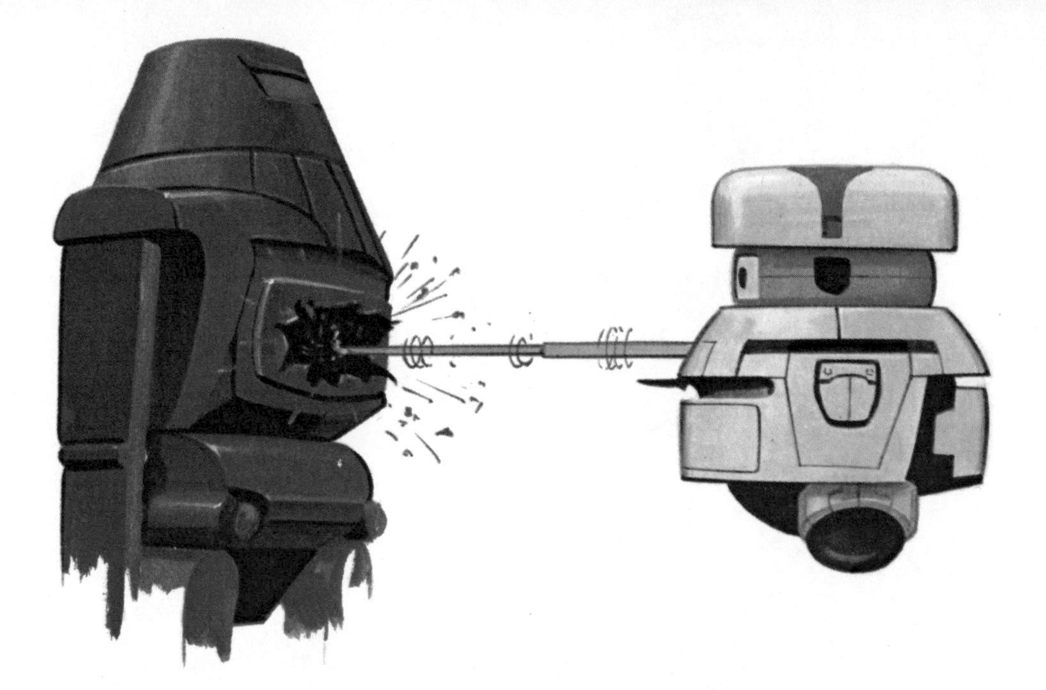

Then V.I.N.CENT. shot out his special cutting arm and cut the wires in Maximillian's control box.

With his wires cut, Maximillian could not work.

He fell to the floor.

V.I.N.CENT. flew out the door and caught up with Dr. Kate and Captain Holland.

Mr. Pizer also found them, and they ran for their lives.

"But where can we go?" asked Dr. Kate.

"To the probe ship!" said V.I.N.CENT.

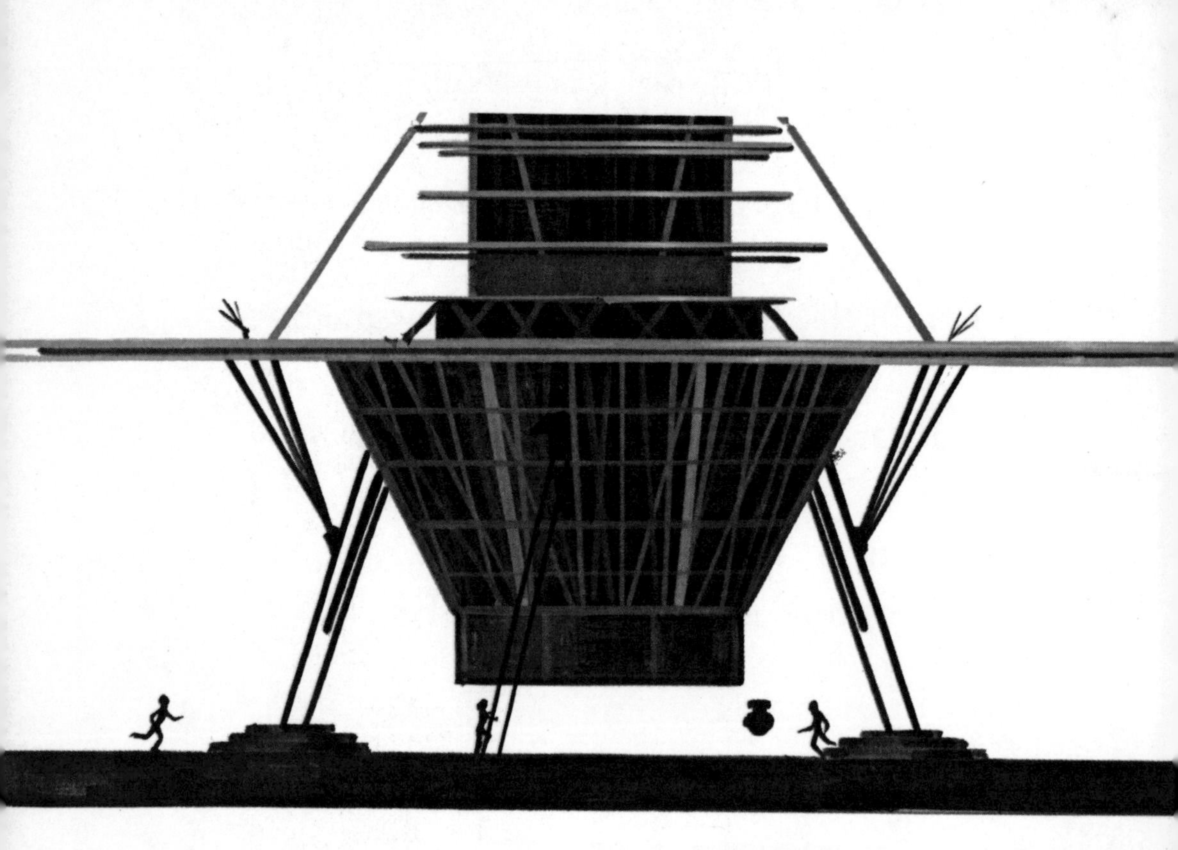

The crew found Dr. Reinhardt's probe ship. They hurried aboard and fired up the rocket engines.

There was a flash of light. It was lift-off!